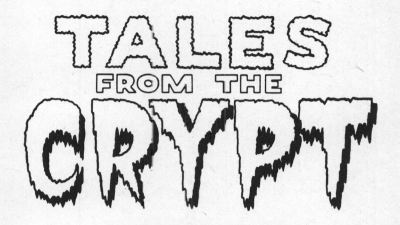

VOLUME 3

Introduced by the Vault-Keeper

Story adaptations by Richard Wenk

Random House New York

The stories in this volume first appeared in different form
in *Tales from the Crypt Comic Books* in the following years:

"Midnight Mess." Copyright 1953 by I. C. Publishing Co., Inc.
Copyright renewed 1981 by William M. Gaines, Agent.

"Voodoo Death." Copyright 1951 by I. C. Publishing Co., Inc.
Copyright renewed 1979 by William M. Gaines, Agent.

"The Trophy." Copyright 1951 by I. C. Publishing Co., Inc.
Copyright renewed 1979 by William M. Gaines, Agent.

"A Sucker for a Spider." Copyright 1952 by I. C. Publishing Co., Inc.
Copyright renewed 1980 by William M. Gaines, Agent.

"Mournin' Ambrose." Copyright 1952 by I. C. Publishing Co., Inc.
Copyright renewed 1980 by William M. Gaines, Agent.

"The Thing from the Grave." Copyright 1950 by I. C. Publishing Co., Inc.
Copyright renewed 1978 by William M. Gaines, Agent.

Library of Congress Cataloging-in-Publication Data
Fremont, Eleanor.   Tales from the crypt. Adaptation of:
   Tales from the crypt. Vol. 3 adapted by Richard Wenk.
   CONTENTS: A collection of horror stories, featuring such grisly
characters as a vampire, werewolf, and murderous madman.
ISBN 0-679-81801-4 (v. 3: pbk.) 1. Horror tales, American.
2. Children's stories, American.   3. Horror stories.   4. Short stories.
I. Gaines, William M. Tales from the crypt.   II. Wenk, Richard.
III. Title. PZ7.W4472Ta1 1991 [Fic] 90-23916

CONTENTS

FROM THE VAULT-KEEPER

 *Welcome, kiddies . . .
Step this way for a friendly
little visit with your old fiend the
Vault-Keeper. Dark and a little
cold down here, isn't it? I like to
keep the candles burning nice and
low. It makes the vault cozy, don't you think?
Besides, you know the awful things that come
out when it gets dark . . .*

Heh! Heh! Nervous?

*Close that door behind you. Just make sure it
doesn't—*

Lock!

*Heh! Heh! Heh! Pound on it all you like! It
won't do any good. Looks like we'll be together
for a while. It's a good thing my Vault of Horror is
packed with my own private collection of the most
revolting tales ever told.*

*What's the matter? Not in the mood for a night
of fright?*

C'mon! Pull up a casket, make yourself comfortable, and we'll see what stories will tickle your frightful fancy. How about "Midnight Mess"? Bet you've never been to a town like the one in _this_ story. It'll make you think twice about _ever_ leaving home.

Then, if you dare, try "Voodoo Death." It's perfect for all you little creepyboppers who think ancient curses and voodoo dolls are just mumbo jumbo.

Or how about "The Trophy"? It takes you on a journey into the wilds of North America, where the deadliest creatures aren't always of the four-legged variety.

Like bugs? Of course you do. And you'll be crawling with fear after reading "A Sucker for a Spider." Hey, what's that on your shoulder? Just kidding. I live to watch people jump. Hand me that bowl of mint cockroaches, will you?

In "Mournin' Ambrose" you'll meet a hideous old couple. Unlucky, too. Seems like just about everyone they meet dies a mysterious death. . . .

And finally a story of love gone bad—real bad: "The Thing from the Grave." If you're squeamish, skip it. If you're the ghastly little ghouls I think you are, you'll eat it up. . . .

So get ready for a night of loathsome literature, kiddies. The horror—I mean, the fun—is about to begin. Don't say I didn't warn you. . . .

Loathsomely yours,
The Vault-Keeper

First stop on our terrifying travels is Oak Bluffs. It's hard to find someone who'll give you directions in this quiet little burg. As a matter of fact, it's hard to find a person at all. Wonder why . . . ?

MIDNIGHT MESS

Before the train's hollow-sounding whistle had faded away, Harold Madison was crossing Oak Bluffs' town square. The clock on the steeple of Town Hall began to chime. It was five o'clock. The sun had already sunk below the row of quaint storefronts, casting long, eerie shadows across the cobblestone walkways. Harold set down his suitcase.

"This is strange," he thought. "No people. No cabs. Nothing!" He wondered again why his sister Donna had taken such a liking to the place. She had moved here a year ago and hadn't been back home since. Harold thought it would be nice to pay her a surprise visit.

"I've never seen a town look so . . . dead," he grumbled.

Suddenly from across the street came the loud clanging of an iron gate being pulled down in front of a store. An old decrepit man locked it, wrapped a string of garlic cloves around his neck, and hurried down the street.

"Excuse me," Harold called after him.

The old man turned his head but didn't break stride. He cast a fear-filled glance at Harold.

"Hey, you!" Harold yelled. "Do you know where 1223 Shore Street is?"

"Shore Street?" The old man slowed down a little. "West for two blocks, then three blocks east," he said. "But you'd better hurry. It's getting dark!"

"Dark? So?" Harold chuckled. "You ever heard of street lamps, old man? Maybe they haven't been invented here yet."

The old man's bloodshot eyes narrowed. He scowled. "You're a stranger here, aren't you?"

Harold nodded.

"Then you don't know about . . . the vampires, do you?" the old man hissed. "Better hurry. It'll be sundown soon. In case you didn't know, vampires come out after sundown!"

Before Harold could say a word, the old man vanished down a narrow alley between two stores, his tattered clothes flapping in the wind. Suddenly the square was empty again.

"Not exactly what I'd call the welcome wagon," commented Harold.

On the next block the flickering of the red neon sign for the Sunny-Side Up restaurant caught his eye. He hadn't eaten a thing since breakfast, and he realized he was very hungry.

The door creaked, and a little bell above it tinkled as Harold entered. The restaurant was small, and except for a couple of people finishing their dinners it was as empty as the rest of Oak Bluffs.

Years ago the place would have seemed elegant. There were only ten tables, and each was draped with a faded and frayed tablecloth. The intricate woodwork was covered with a layer of dust. A mirror covering the entire back wall of the restaurant made it look much bigger than it really was.

Harold sat down and a waiter appeared at his table. The old man's half-glasses barely clung to the tip of his nose, and only the faintest wisps of gray hair ringed his bony head. In contrast to the man Harold had met in the street, the waiter had friendly eyes.

"Listen, gimme a ham and—" Harold began.

But the waiter cut him off. "I'm sorry, sir, we're closing," he said. He reached down and switched off the small lamp on Harold's table. "I must ask you to leave. It's almost dark, you know."

Harold's jaw dropped. "What's with you

people and darkness?" he exclaimed.

"As a courtesy to our employees, we close early so they can get home before sundown," the waiter stated. "The vampires, you know."

"Vampires?" Harold exclaimed. "Whew! This is the nuttiest town I've ever been to."

"Obviously you haven't heard about the horrible things happening here," the waiter said. He pulled out a chair and sat his tired body down across from Harold. "There have been seventeen bodies found in Oak Bluffs over the last two years with every drop of blood drained from them."

Harold's look was skeptical. It sounded

gruesome, all right, but vampires? Ridiculous.

"The whole town has been in the grip of fear since shortly after the . . . murders began," the waiter continued. "Each body had a hole in its neck, and not a drop of blood was left. What else could have done such a deed?"

"Hey, I don't know," Harold said impatiently. "But how about a ham sandwich, pal? Or an omelet?"

The waiter stood up. He got Harold's coat from the rack and handed it to him. Then he pushed him toward the door.

"Crazy or not, I suggest that you get to where you're going before dark," the waiter said. "When darkness comes, the vampires roam the streets looking for victims. Don't let one of them be you!" He opened the door.

Harold left feeling hungry and confused. Was everyone in this town crazy? He wondered if Donna believed in the vampires too, then decided it was impossible. Living in a little burg like Oak Bluffs wouldn't make her mind go soft. Not a chance.

A few minutes later Harold was marching down Shore Street, peering at house numbers through the gloomy darkness, listening to the sound of doors being slammed and bolted tight, windows being closed and shuttered. The wind had picked up and was playing a haunting melody through the gnarled and twisted branches of the trees.

Finally he found his sister's home. It was a big old Victorian-style house at the end of the street, and it was dark. An old rocking chair on the front porch swayed back and forth in the wind, creaking loudly. Dried-up leaves skittered across the porch.

Harold knocked. The porch light came on.

"Who is it?" Donna called from inside.

"Donna, it's me!" Harold shouted through the whistling gusts of wind. "Your brother."

Donna threw open the door and grabbed Harold by the hand, pulling him inside. "What are you doing out in the dark?" she cried. She gave Harold a huge hug.

Harold dropped his suitcase and frowned.

"You believe in this vampire garbage too?" he moaned.

Donna locked the door and led Harold through the foyer into the living room. "What are you doing here?" she asked. "I wish you

had called." She took his coat and sat him down.

"I'm on my way up the coast to a dental association conference," he replied. "I'm president this year."

"That's wonderful," Donna said with little enthusiasm.

"What's going on around here?" Harold demanded. "This whole town is shaking in its boots, including you."

"Something awful is happening in Oak

Bluffs," Donna said. Harold hadn't seen her look so frightened since the night of her senior prom, when he had hidden a garter snake in her purse.

"*Vampires?*" Harold snorted.

"What else could it be?" she asked, her eyes wide. "Seventeen villagers murdered, their bodies—"

"There are dozens of possible explanations," Harold said, wishing she could see how crazy it was to believe in such nonsense. "There could be a homicidal maniac loose. Or—"

"Believe what you want to believe, Harold," said Donna. "I bet you're tired. I'll show you to your room. We can talk in the morning."

Despite the fact that all was quiet, Harold couldn't fall asleep. When the old grandfather clock in the hallway chimed twelve, he decided to go for a walk.

He dressed quickly, threw on his coat, and sneaked out the front door. He hoped Donna didn't hear him leaving. She obviously believed in that vampire stuff. Just knowing he was out in the night would scare her.

All was quiet until Harold turned a corner

a block from the town square. In the distance he heard people talking and laughing. Somewhere up ahead a crowd of people was having a good time.

Harold briskly walked toward the square. When he got there, he couldn't believe his eyes. The Sunny-Side Up restaurant was open! The red neon sign was blinking merrily, and people were coming and going. Each time the door opened loud laughter and chatter escaped into the moonless night.

"That old waiter lied to me," Harold said to himself. "Amazing."

Inside the restaurant the mood was festive. Almost every table was filled with people talking, laughing, drinking, and eating. Harold headed for a table near the far wall. Everyone smiled and raised their glasses as he passed by.

"Finally! Some normal people!" Harold thought.

"Will you be having dinner, sir?" asked a waiter. He was different from the one Harold had spoken to earlier.

"What's the special tonight?"

"Juice, soup, roast with French fries, coffee, and sherbet," the waiter recited.

"Cook it up and send it my way," Harold said.

Harold was starved by the time his tomato juice finally arrived. To his dismay, it was thin and salty. He had to force himself to finish what was in the glass.

"What kind of tomato juice *is* this?" he asked.

The waiter grinned. "Very funny, sir," he said.

The soup was even saltier and stranger tasting than the juice. Harold began having second thoughts about his meal. Suddenly going hungry didn't seem so bad.

"Hey, waiter, listen—"

"How would you like your roast clots, sir? Well-done or medium?" the waiter interrupted.

"Roast *what?*" Harold cried, spitting out a mouthful of soup.

"Roast blood clots, of course," the waiter said. Then his expression changed. "Say, who are you?" he asked suspiciously.

Harold rose, feeling queasy.

"Draw the curtain!" the waiter growled to the rest of the patrons. "There's an intruder in our midst!"

Several people pulled aside the curtain that covered the big mirror on the back wall of the restaurant. Harold saw himself in the mirror. Only himself. The blood drained from his face.

"You people are . . ." He turned, unable to continue, and found himself surrounded by . . . vampires, their eyes bloodshot, their fangs glinting. They were the most horrible creatures he'd ever seen.

"Harold!" someone shouted.

Donna suddenly stood before him.

"I told you not to come out at night," she scolded. "Why didn't you do as I said?"

"Donna, I'm so glad you're here," Harold

sobbed. "You've got to get us out of here. These . . . things are looking at me like I'm some kind of steak!"

"You don't understand, do you?" Donna said. "I'm one of them! I'm a vampire too."

"You . . . ?" Harold whimpered.

"Why do you think I came to this town and stayed here?" she asked. "This is the one place I could go."

Harold's head was spinning. "But this restaurant . . ." he wondered out loud. "I don't understand. . . ."

"In the old days humans hunted and prepared their own food," she explained. "But now we vampires leave the hunting to the professionals. We leave the preparing to the professionals, too.

"This restaurant serves blood dishes just the way a vegetarian restaurant serves vegetable dishes," she added. "Blood juice cocktail. Hot blood consommé. Roast blood clots . . ."

Harold gagged. The thought of eating such disgusting things repulsed him. And to think he had gulped down a large order of blood juice cocktail.

"Can't you let me go?" he pleaded. "I'm

your brother. Don't you remember?"

"I'm sorry, Harold," said Donna. "Like the others, you will have to be silenced. I cannot save you. You should have stayed in the city like a good dentist."

"A dentist?" said a hideous-looking man. "Listen, Doc, before we . . . uh, how shall I say it . . . dine with you . . . do you think there's anything you can do with these fangs?" His skin was so white Harold could see the blue blood pumping through the veins in his face. "I'd like to make them longer. To get a better . . . grip on the situation. Know what I mean?"

Harold looked for a way out. Suddenly the waiter yelled, "String him up!"

The vampires jerked Harold off his feet and carried him into the kitchen. They tied his hands and legs and hung him upside down from a large hook in the ceiling.

"Get the tap!" one of them called.

Carl, the cook, handled the tap. It took a great deal of skill to insert it into the victim's neck correctly, without spilling a drop. Carl was three hundred and twenty-five years old and had more experience than most in these matters.

"Okay, Carl, screw it into his neck!" everyone shouted.

Squishhhhhhh.

Harold Madison's wild screams quickly turned to a pathetic gurgling.

"I'm first!" cried one of the vampires. He stepped up and pulled the tap handle.

Harold's blood, thick and hot, flowed from the tap into the vampire's glass. He took a big gulp.

"Ahh," he said dreamily. "Nothing like the fresh stuff."

One by one the vampires filled their glasses to the brim, and one by one they lifted them high in the air.

"A toast to my brother Harold," Donna said, facing the crowd. "Good to the last drop. . . ."

Guess old Harold should have ordered a stake! But how could he know he'd found a true-blue blooditarian restaurant?

It does warm my cold heart to see a roomful of vampires having a snack attack. Remember, the next time you visit Oak Bluffs, no nipping the waiters!

Feeling a little queasy yet? No? This next tale of gore should take care of that! It's proof that the most deadly things do come in small packages. . . .

VOODOO DEATH

"C'mon, Bill, you know this is wrong—dead wrong!" Jay whispered as he trailed Bill Randall through the steamy overgrown Haitian jungle. Smack in the middle of this sweltering island was the last place Jay wanted to be. He had been slimed, bitten, and crawled upon by just about every eight-legged creature in the jungle—and the nearest road was more than an hour away.

"Don't tell me what's right or wrong!" snapped Bill. Dressed in a khaki shirt and pants, a wide-brimmed hat, and hiking boots, Bill looked every inch the archaeologist. Although his father had been a world-famous historian and scientist, Bill had inherited little of his father's thirst for understanding ancient cultures. What *he* wanted was fame and fortune. So far both had eluded him, but he would stop at nothing until he had both in his grasp.

"You just keep an eye out for stray natives," Bill growled. "They're known to kill outsiders who try to interfere with their pagan rituals. Don't be such a wimp! You know what your problem is? You don't have any heart."

"These people are entitled to live their lives without any interference from us," said Jay. "All this talk about stealing a sacred voodoo doll gives me the creeps. Your father's probably turning over in his grave."

Bill waved his hand to silence Jay. They crept up a hill, parted a tangle of thick branches, and peered down into a clearing.

Far below, a ring of natives danced around a dead body lying on the ground. It lay inside a circle of dead lizards and vulture bones and was covered with strange-looking leaves and flowers. The sound of drums thundering through the hot, thick air terrified Jay.

"Wh-what are they doing?" he stammered.

"He's the native who was shot to death in town yesterday," said Bill. "They're working over him."

A high priestess wearing a turban and a long dress made of animal skins approached the body. The drums beat louder and the dancing became wilder. She knelt down, bowed in front of the corpse, and began speaking to it.

"Part of an ancient voodoo ritual," Bill explained.

When she was finished, she placed a tiny voodoo doll alongside the body. A long razor-sharp pin held the ragged doll together.

Suddenly the chanting stopped. A deadly stillness fell over the clearing. The high priestess stood above the corpse as the rest of the natives moved away, staring intently as their spiritual leader waved her hands and chanted softly.

Then, to Jay's utter horror, the corpse began to shake. Its eyes flashed open, glassy and empty. Then it lifted itself off the ground and stood, staring blankly into the night.

The high priestess raised her arms to the sky, and suddenly the tiny voodoo doll rose up alongside the zombielike corpse. Before Bill or Jay could blink, the doll darted past the circle of natives and into the darkness of the jungle.

"Did you see that?" Jay cried, his eyes wide with fright. "The dead man! He's alive. He—"

"Shut up, you fool!" hissed Bill. "They'll hear you!"

But it was too late. The natives had heard Jay's voice. They quickly turned and pointed at the intruders, gesturing and shouting wildly. The high priestess barked an angry command, and in an instant the natives were racing right for them!

"Run!" Bill screamed.

Jay turned. The natives were at the edge of the clearing and gaining fast. He pumped his legs furiously but went nowhere. To his horror, the loose dirt gave out from under him, and before he knew it, he was lying flat on his face.

In the next instant he was surrounded. He kicked and struggled with every ounce of strength he had, but it was no use. His arms and legs were pinned to his sides.

"Bill, come back!" Jay screamed. "They've got me, Bill! Don't leave me! Help!"

Bill heard Jay's awful cries as he scrambled through the darkness and the vines. But he did not turn back.

Glaring down at Jay with anger in their eyes, the natives waited for their leader to tell them what to do next.

Jay smiled meekly at his captors, hoping a little friendliness would go a long way. It didn't.

The high priestess roared an angry command and he was carried away.

Back at the hotel Bill packed furiously. A steamship was scheduled to leave Port-au-Prince early that morning, and he was determined to be on it. The tiny hotel room was hot, and the ceiling fan provided little relief from the heat.

"That fool!" Bill mumbled, mopping sweat

from his brow. "It was his own fault. In the jungle it's every man for himself. Besides, he was a worthless—"

"Leaving so soon, Bill?"

Bill turned. To his horror, Jay stood before him. He looked dazed.

"Jay?" Bill exclaimed. "Th-thank God, you escaped. I . . . I . . . was just going to get the police to go back and find you . . . and . . ."

Jay collapsed on the bed, holding his head. "Voodoo doll," he muttered wearily. His words were slurred and flat. "Voodoo . . . zombie . . ."

"What are you talking about?" asked Bill.

"Heart . . . voodoo doll . . ." Jay rambled.

Bill shook his head. "That's just what I need, some kind of loony partner," he grumbled. "Look, we'll both get on the next boat out of here. Get a good night's sleep."

From the steamer's bow the mysterious island of Haiti became just a tiny speck on the horizon as Bill and Jay watched. They were happy to be sailing for New York and relieved that their terrible ordeal was behind them.

After dinner, Bill said good night to Jay and headed for bed. Entering his cabin, he threw his

jacket on a chair and flipped on the bedside light.

"What the—" he said, shuddering.

A tiny voodoo doll exactly like the one from the jungle ceremony sat slumped against his pillow, a huge, ugly needle clasped in front of its body.

Suddenly it bent forward and rose to its feet. Bill stumbled back in horror.

"The natives must have sent a doll after me!" he realized. "It must be a punishment for witnessing their sacred ritual. They're trying to kill me!"

Bill moved quickly. He scooped up the evil-looking doll, pulled open the porthole of his cabin, and hurled the doll into the night.

"Bill, what's happening in here?" Jay said, standing in the doorway.

"The voodoo doll, Jay!" Bill cried. "The natives are angry because I saw their ritual. They're trying to kill me!"

"You've been in the sun too long, old buddy," Jay said. "You're seeing things."

Bill's hands shook as he lit a cigarette. "I don't know," he said. "It looked at me like I was a human pincushion!"

"Maybe now you're the one who needs some sleep," said Jay. "Everything will be all right once we get back to New York."

And everything did seem to be all right, until about two weeks later. . . .

Then, late one night Bill heard a tapping at the door. Jay had gone out for the evening and Bill was alone in the apartment they shared. He opened the door, but no one was there, just a package wrapped in brown paper. No return address. No postmark. He hastily unwrapped the package, lifted the lid, and . . .

He dropped the box on the floor and stumbled back in horror.

The voodoo doll was stuffed inside. It

seemed to be taunting him with a devilish grin. "Thought you were rid of me, eh?" he could almost hear it sneering. The long needle it held was razor sharp and gleamed wickedly in the light.

Panic-stricken, Bill tossed the box and its grotesque contents into the fireplace. As the box curled up in flames, Bill went into his study to pour himself a drink. Suddenly a frightening thought occurred to him. If that . . . thing . . . could come back after being thrown into the ocean, couldn't it escape the fire somehow?

He ran back to the fireplace. The box had been reduced to ashes, but the doll was gone!

"Where are you?" Bill screamed, turning every which way, hoping to see the doll before it was upon him. "I know you're in here! Come out and fight like a doll!"

"Bill, what's going on?" Jay demanded as he burst through the door. He had heard Bill's ranting and raving from down the hall. "Have you gone completely nuts?"

· "It's back, Jay. It's here in this room, hiding, waiting to kill me!"

"Let me guess, Bill," Jay said calmly. "A little dude, six inches tall, carrying a long

menácing-looking needle? Something that could go right through your heart?"

"That's him!" Bill cried. "Have you seen it, Jay?"

"Can't say that I have, Bill."

"Why are you so calm about this?" Bill said, glaring at Jay. "You think it's just after me? He'll kill you, too."

"I've already paid the price for our little adventure," Jay said. "You were dead right when you said they didn't like outsiders witnessing their sacred voodoo rituals. I'm telling you, Bill, they don't just get mad, they get even!"

"What are you talking about?"

Jay glanced at the ceiling. "Hey, Bill, what's that in the chandelier?"

Bill craned his head. A scream tried to escape his throat as the voodoo doll leaped from the chandelier and dropped onto his shoulder, the long needle plunging painfully into his neck.

"Get it off me! *Aaahhh!*" he screamed as the needle sunk in deeper.

In an instant the voodoo doll slumped over. Bill pulled it off his shoulder and threw it to the floor. The doll lay there limp and lifeless.

"Heh! Heh!" Bill giggled with nervous relief. "It jabbed me and then croaked. Went to that big dollhouse in the sky . . ." Before he could finish, his neck began to go numb. In seconds his whole body ached with a terrible pain. "I'm getting weaker—"

"These little guys get right to the point, don't they?" Jay said with a sinister snicker. "The needle was poisoned. Soon your whole body will hurt, Bill, and then you'll be dead. . . . As dead as I am."

"Dead as—"

"That's right, I'm dead," Jay said, his eyes shining with an evil glow. "After you ran off and left me in that jungle, the natives taught me a lesson in good manners. They sent me and the doll back to punish you. You're about to die, Bill, old boy!"

Bill's anger suddenly rose. The little monster was about to take his life, just as he was on the verge of greatness! He grabbed the doll and viciously ripped it in half. Something tumbled out of the old cloth that held the figure together. He picked it up. It was dripping.

"Good lord, it's a heart!" he shrieked in disgust. "A human heart."

"That's right, Bill," Jay said, ripping open his own shirt and exposing a huge scar stitched crudely across his chest. "They gave it *my* heart!"

Bill and Jay slumped down on the floor. Bill moaned and shivered in pain as the poison coursed through his veins. It wouldn't be long before both of them had paid the price for going where they didn't belong. . . .

A heartrending story, eh? Poor Bill, his search for the voodoo doll was all in vein. But in my next terrifying tale you'll meet someone who always gets his prey. . . .

 *Had enough? No? That's what I like—gluttons for punishment! The next story is about a hunting expedition that gets turned on its head. Happy haunting, er, hunting, kiddies. . . .*

THE TROPHY

What did I see in the eyes of the man who had just entered the dimly lit room? Horror? Pity? Disgust? Or was it amusement at the very sight of what had become of me?

"What are you looking at, huh? You think it's funny, is that it?"

The man mumbled something I couldn't hear. The ceaseless gurgling of the machinery and the utter drone of air being pumped through bellows drowned out all but the loudest of noises.

I let out a laugh that cut through the noise and sent the man reeling backward. The look on his face left nothing to the imagination. It was horror—pure and simple.

"Take a seat," I said once the man had

calmed down. "Got a cigarette? Never mind. I've got a little story to tell you. My name is Clyde Franklin. Perhaps you've heard of me? Anyway, I was about to leave for one of my extravagant—and always successful—hunting expeditions . . ."

There was an early chill in the air that fall. The urge to add another trophy to my wall had overtaken me. I decided an excursion into the wilderness of North America was in order.

"Take care of things around here, Jeeves," I told my trusty servant as I climbed into the fully loaded station wagon. "I'll bring a moose head back just for you, old boy."

Jeeves bid me good luck and I was off. The Alaska Highway would lead me to one of the most glorious places on earth. The air was crystal clear, the lakes and streams glittered in the sunlight, and across the land roamed enough game to keep a crusty old hunter like me happy.

On this trip I planned to hunt caribou, puma, moose, or any other unfortunate animal that might cross my gun sights. I had the reputation as one of the most fearless hunters alive—ever to have lived, if you ask me. I've stalked caribou in the farthest reaches of North America; elephants and the deadly jaguar in the deepest, darkest parts of Africa. There isn't a man alive who's encountered the icy face of death as often as I and come away with a trophy that would make any hunter proud.

And trophies were what I was after—heads, actually. Some fools claim that hunting poor defenseless animals is cruel. Nonsense! Denying a man his sport is what's cruel, if you ask me.

After ten hours of nonstop driving, I reached an out-of-the-way clearing alongside a little stream. I pitched my tent and watched the sun sink slowly in the sky. In the morning I would make my way into the woods and undoubtedly come away with another trophy for my wall.

I always did.

That morning was no exception. I tracked an enormous moose through the thick trees for more than three hours. Finally I was close enough. The moose, whose antlers were perhaps the most majestic I'd ever seen, stood placidly drinking in a shallow stream. I stared for a moment at the fantastic creature. What an addition to my wall he would make!

I raised my gun, centered him in my sights, and pulled the trigger.

Boom!

In one sudden motion the great moose fell to his knees. He raised his head and boldly stared at me, a certain sadness in those big brown eyes.

Then the stubborn moose snorted and rose from his knees. "A feisty one," I thought, and chuckled. I always enjoyed a good fight. His bellow echoed through the crisp, thin air, and before I knew it he was galloping straight for me.

I stood my ground. The gigantic animal, wild with deadly thoughts of survival and vengeance, pounded his hoofs into the dirt with every ounce of his remaining strength.

Again I raised my gun, placing him squarely in the cross hairs. The furious animal grew closer. Getting run over by a stampeding moose would be like getting hit by a truck. He would most certainly crush me. Still I waited. Waited until I had that vital spot in my sights . . .

. . . then pulled the trigger.

Crack! The shot cut through the still morn-ing air.

The moose dropped like a fallen tree not more than three feet in front of me. He was dead.

Luckily for me he hadn't broken his antlers when he toppled. Yes, indeed. He was going to make a fine addition to my trophy room.

The next day I broke camp and headed deeper into the wilderness. After a hundred more miles on a narrow pass through the snow-covered mountains, I decided to stop for gas.

"Fill 'er up," I said to the attendant.

"That's a mighty impressive moose head you have there, mister," he drawled after spying my magnificent trophy in the back of the station wagon. "Where's the carcass? An animal that size could feed a family up here all winter."

"I never planned on eating it," I said with disgust.

"Shucks," he whined. "People 'round here hunt so's they can eat. That's a lot of food gone to waste."

"I don't hunt for *food*," I snarled. "I hunt for *sport!*"

I pulled out of the gas station with a squeal of my tires and headed up the lonely, twisting mountain road. I drove steadily for several hours. Then, just as night fell, it happened. My headlights illuminated a board studded with huge spikes. To my dismay I saw that the board stretched clear across the road.

I hit the brakes as hard as I could. The tires let out an earsplitting screech and billows of white smoke shot out from beneath the car.

It was too late. The front tires exploded with a deafening *boom*, and suddenly the car

spun out of control. It swerved with a mind of its own—right toward the edge of the cliff.

"Noooooooooo!" I screamed.

The wildly spinning car burst through the weathered guardrails and tumbled over the side of the mountain. Metal crunching against the snowy rocks, glass shattering in every direction, the engine bursting into flames, were the last dreadful sounds I heard before everything went black. . . .

When I finally came to—sprawled on a flimsy cot in a rustic old cabin—I couldn't decide which part of my body hurt more. My head was throbbing, and my leg ached with a pain I had never felt before. I could barely keep myself from passing out.

From somewhere outside the cabin I heard voices and the strange sound of a machine pumping away. Soon I could make out the voices more clearly. I didn't like what I heard.

"Please don't!" came the bloodcurdling cry of a man. "Have mercy on me! Don't hurt me! Don't hurt me!"

I struggled to rise from the musty cot only to discover that my leg had been badly broken—snapped at the knee. There was no way I could walk, much less save the man who was screaming. I lay back on the cot, barely conscious, writhing in pain.

Soon the screaming faded to a horrible gurgling moan. Then the cabin door opened, and someone stood in the doorway watching me. Behind him I saw an old shack in a clearing. It sounded as though the noise from the machine was coming from the shack.

"Ah! You've come around," the old man said quietly. He stepped into the cabin and approached, wringing his gnarled and scarred hands. He stared at me from the foot of the cot through bloodshot eyes. "How do you feel?" he asked. "I was afraid you might have a concussion."

"What do *you* think?" I snapped. "Look at this leg! I'm in pain. I need a doctor! Now!"

He looked at me gleefully. "I'm not interested in your leg!" he said.

I was amazed, then angry. "What kind of man are you?" I demanded. "Who do you have in there? It sounds like you're torturing him."

The man nodded. "You heard, eh?"

"Yes, I heard. But look, you've got to set my leg or get me to a doctor."

"You're not going anywhere," the man said. "You're my . . . prisoner."

He began to chuckle with sinister delight. It was then that I knew.

"The spikes! It was you who put the board across the road!" I exclaimed.

"You catch on quickly," he said, smiling coldly. "Let us say that I 'bagged' you, as a hunter bags an animal."

He turned and started out.

"What are you going to do to me?" I screamed.

His last words were, "You'll see. . . . You'll see. . . ."

I sat alone in the room for more than an hour. The constant drone of the machinery from the shack across the clearing—and the constant moaning of whoever was being tortured in there—began to torture *me*. I had to see what was going on in there. Besides, I knew that maniac was planning on doing something awful to me. I prayed that there would be a phone in that little shack. Maybe, just maybe, I could save myself.

I struggled off the cot and dragged myself to the door. Luckily the old man had left it unlocked. I managed to hop over to the shack. I paused at the door, wondering what it was that I would see in there.

The door creaked as it swung open. Sunlight flooded in. My heart pounded fiercely. What was I about to see? A horribly mutilated body? No. I found . . .

Nothing.

The room was empty except for a long white table with something that looked like a cake box on top. And there was a strange machine sitting next to the table, connected to it by all sorts of bubbling tubes. The machine seemed to be pumping something underneath the table straight up to that box—liquids of some sort.

I hobbled painfully into the room and headed straight for that box. Standing closer now, I realized that it was not a box at all. It was a metal cover. Something was under it.

My hand was about to lift the cover when I suddenly froze in a flood of fear. A bloodcurdling moan . . . a horrible, sad, and pathetic groan . . . escaped from beneath it!

I raised the metal cover and went limp. It fell to the floor with a clang.

There on the table before me was the most horrifying sight I had ever seen. It was a living, breathing human head! Its eyes blinked, and then in obvious pain it began to speak.

"Get out of here," it moaned. "Run, you fool! He's mad! He'll get you, too! Run while you can!"

I stood paralyzed, rooted in place by fear. It was as though I were numb from head to toe.

"Ah, I see you discovered my trophy room!"

The old man stood blocking the doorway. Then he shut the door behind him and locked it.

"Your *what?*" I said, stunned.

The man smiled. He looked even more hideous than before.

"My trophy room. This is where I keep the heads of all of my game," he said.

He turned and took a can off a shelf behind him.

"You're crazy! You can't hunt human beings!"

"Why not?" he growled. "I hunt for the sport of it."

"Sport!" I cried. "It's . . . it's murder!"

"Call it what you will," the insane old man roared as he reached for a sponge. "One man's sport is another man's murder."

He drenched the sponge with the liquid from the can and came at me. I turned to run, but my broken leg sent me sprawling. In an instant he was over me, shoving the dripping sponge toward my face.

Sickened by the odor of chloroform, I struggled to get away, but the drug soon took effect. My mind began to drift. My body suddenly felt like it was floating away into the darkness . . .

I saw the old man's ugly face staring down at me. The last thing I heard him say was . . .

"After all, they're only human beings."

Pretty story, eh? Now I—Clyde Franklin, one of the greatest hunters ever to have lived—am one of his prized trophies. Doomed to a life of looking out over this tabletop, listening to the horrible throbbing noise of the machine that keeps my head alive, looking forward to the days when he comes in with another . . . catch.

"Now, my friend, how about that cigarette?"

Poor Clyde! Guess he won't have to pay attention to the Surgeon General's warning on the cigarette pack, eh? Lung cancer isn't a worry of his anymore. . . .

Okay, you little insect lovers, put away your pet tarantulas! Here's a slithering saga of greedy gore! If this horrifying tale doesn't get your skin creeping and crawling, my name isn't the Vault-Keeper. So sit back, relax, and let yourself be paralyzed with fear. You might just become . . .

A SUCKER FOR A SPIDER

Randolph Spurd had hoped to make it quick. He had something very important to say, but his boss, Maxwell Stoneman, president of the County Bank and Trust Company, had talked nonstop the entire evening.

"Come on, Randolph, before we have our coffee, I'd like to show you something *really* interesting," Stoneman said, lifting his considerable bulk from the chair. "I have rare and exotic spiders from all over the world. Been my hobby for years."

"Ah, Mr. Stoneman," Randolph began

weakly. "There's some very important business I want to—"

"Save it, Randolph," Stoneman interrupted the bank teller. "Follow me."

Randolph rose from the long dinner table and trailed his boss through the mansion to the entrance of a glass-walled greenhouse.

The sun had gone down hours ago, but the greenhouse was stiflingly hot and muggy. Cov-

ering one wall of the room was a row of glass cases. Each case contained a thick patch of dirt from which moist green foliage sprouted.

"Fascinating creatures, spiders. I can spend hours out here just watching them creep around. I love 'em, Spurd."

"They're certainly, uhm . . . interesting, Mr. Stoneman," Spurd said. "Now, about that business—"

"This one's a tarantula," said Stoneman, pointing to a huge, hairy eight-legged creature crouched on a dripping leaf.

"Is it poisonous?" Randolph gulped.

"No! The black widow's the only spider found in the United States that can kill a human being," Stoneman said.

They stopped in front of another, larger case. Inside a perfectly formed web, like a delicate bull's-eye, was spun between several twigs. A monstrous black and brown spider sat poised on the edge of a leaf, watching its web intently.

"I'm horribly frightened of spiders," Spurd said. "Do you think, perhaps, we might be able to talk business—"

"This big son of a gun is a vermula spider," Stoneman interrupted again. "A very rare species. Take a look at what the vermula does to one of its victims. It's incredible!"

He reached below the spider case and brought up a bottle whose top was covered with cheesecloth. Flies buzzed frantically around inside. Stoneman captured one of the flies, opened the case, and flung it into the vermula's web.

"See how the little fellow sticks there!" Stoneman cackled sadistically. "The thing's struggling to free itself—all in vain. The vermula's web is covered with an adhesive coating," he added with increasing glee.

"Mr. Stoneman—please!" cried Spurd.

With amazing speed the spider crawled across the delicate rungs of the web toward the struggling insect.

"See how the vermula sinks its fangs into the fly? It paralyzes its victims," Stoneman said with a chuckle. "Then it spins a covering around it. See how it turns the fly over as it spins its cocoon?"

Randolph grimaced. He hadn't come here to see flies being tortured.

"The fly's still alive!" he said. "Wrapped in that sticky—"

"That's right!" Stoneman exclaimed. "The vermula will keep the fly that way until it's ready to eat. Then it will inject the fly with an enzyme that acts as a predigestion agent. It merely sucks up the liquefied insides of the fly, leaving only the dry outer shell. Ha, ha, ha! Fascinating, isn't it?"

"It's revolting!" Randolph said.

"You sound shocked, Randolph."

"I am. I think it's cruel to throw those poor flies into that viscous spider's web!"

"That's nature—dog-eat-dog, or in this case spider-eat-fly! That's the way it survives. We all have to do whatever it takes to survive, don't we, Randolph?

"Maybe you're right," the teller replied thoughtfully.

He followed his boss through the greenhouse and back into the luxurious living room.

"All right, Randolph," Stoneman said finally. "What's on your mind?"

"Well, sir, I—I've noticed something wrong at the bank. Something terribly wrong . . ."

"Oh?"

"It's the books, sir. They don't balance,"

Spurd continued. "In fact, it's obvious to me that someone is stealing from the bank. And I know who that someone is."

"You . . . you do?" Now Stoneman was watching Spurd very carefully.

Randolph nodded. "When I came here to-night I intended to tell you about the theft so you could replace the money you stole. I wasn't going to say a thing. . . ."

Maxwell Stoneman scowled. "Are you accusing me?" he snapped.

From outside a flash of lightning lit up the entire living room, followed a split second later by a thunderous crack! Then sheets of rain began to pelt the tall windows.

"After hearing your talk tonight," said the teller, "about dog-eat-dog, I've decided that I could forget I noticed anything . . ."

Stoneman regarded Randolph suspiciously. "Really?" he asked.

"For, say, five thousand dollars," Spurd continued. "That isn't asking too much, is it? Compared with *fifty-two thousand?*"

"So that's your plan, eh? Blackmail."

"Let's call it a struggle to survive, sir," Spurd replied. "You pay me and you survive.

Just like you said—it's nature."

Stoneman stared silently at his feeble-looking chief teller. Then he began to laugh, harder and harder. His guffaws echoed through the mansion.

"You win, Randolph," he said, at last. "I'm proud of you! I didn't think you had it in you. Five grand? Okay, it's a deal."

"And I get to keep my job. That's in the deal too," Randolph said, suddenly feeling unsure about what he was doing. Could it be this easy?

"Of course!" said Stoneman. "No hard feelings. You trapped me like that fly, Randolph. You won."

"Good. Then I'll be going."

Stoneman placed a fleshy arm around his employee's shoulder. "Don't be crazy. There's a terrible storm going on out there. Stay the night. We'll drive in to work together in the morning."

"Well . . ."

"Don't worry, Randolph," Stoneman said, noticing his employee's anxiety. "I'm not going to try anything. I'd be a fool. I'm sure you've got this whole thing documented. If anything happens to you, the authorities will find out about me anyway. Isn't that right?"

"Th-that's right," Spurd muttered, hoping he sounded convincing. Actually, he hadn't even told his wife about it. "All right, I'll stay."

The big grandfather clock in the living room had just struck three when Maxwell Stoneman's shadowy figure crossed the living room from the greenhouse. The storm was still rumbling outside, and the steady patter of rain was loud against the windows.

Stoneman crept silently up the staircase. He reached the landing, turned right, and followed the darkened hallway to the last bedroom. He paused, his ear pressed lightly against the wooden door, listening.

"You think you've got me trapped, eh, Spurd?" Stoneman grumbled to himself. "You'll keep blackmailing me until you suck me dry like the vermula spider will suck that fly dry."

Stoneman slowly turned the door handle and quietly entered the room. Randolph snored beneath the heavy quilts, oblivious to both the thunderstorm and to the man in his room.

"I'm not going to let you suck me dry,

Spurd, you no-good, lousy little penny-counter! I promised I wouldn't do anything to you, but I didn't say anything about one of my spiders—one of my black widow spiders at that!" Stoneman thought.

He slid open the lid of a container and shook the small but deadly spider underneath the covers of Randolph's bed.

"I've aggravated and tormented you, little black widow." Stoneman chuckled to himself. "Take your anger out on him!"

Randolph turned restlessly in bed. The deadly spider crawled out onto the bright-colored quilt. Stoneman gave the blanket an

impatient tug, and the spider's eight delicate limbs propelled it toward the pillow and the warm, steady breath of Randolph Spurd. It stopped at the very edge of the quilt and peered down at Randolph's closed eyes and slightly open mouth. Then the lethal creature took a step forward and tumbled onto the soft flesh of Randolph's neck.

Stoneman had barely closed the bedroom door when an earsplitting scream pierced the night.

"The doctor says a black widow spider killed the poor guy," a detective said early the next morning. "Any idea how the spider got out of its case, Mr. Stoneman?"

Stoneman dabbed at his eyes with a large handkerchief. He had called the police first thing in the morning, saying that one of his employees had died mysteriously in the night. Tears ran down his cheeks even as the detectives searched the room for clues.

"I showed Randolph my spider collection last night," he sobbed. "Maybe one of the case doors had been left slightly ajar. I don't know. It's just terrible . . ."

Randolph's body, covered by a thin white sheet, lay on the bed. Police investigators were going over every inch of the room.

"I invited him to my house socially," Stoneman continued. "I do that often for my employees. I like them to feel that I'm their friend as well as their boss." At this, Stoneman broke down again. Out of the corner of his eye he saw a detective watching him. Obviously the man was not completely convinced of Stoneman's innocence.

"That'll be all for now, Mr. Stoneman," the detective said. "We'll be in touch if we have any more questions."

But Stoneman wasn't taking any chances.

He decided to go to Florida for a couple of months—no sense answering questions if you didn't have to.

Later that afternoon Stoneman was flying his own twin-engine plane high over Georgia, laughing at the stupidity of the police and his own chief teller, the extremely dead Randolph Spurd.

"That's the Okefenokee Swamp," he said,

peering through an opening in the clouds. "I'm just two hours from Miami."

Suddenly the plane's engine sputtered and coughed. Its control panel lit up like a pinball machine. Though Stoneman flicked all the right switches, the plane started to dive, heading almost straight down through the clouds.

Stoneman frantically unbuckled his seat belt. He threw on a parachute pack, thrust open the door, and leaped from the plane. He pulled the cord. The chute mushroomed open and he fell silently, lazily toward the ground.

The Okefenokee Swamp, with its thickly overgrown trees, marshes, and tangles of vines, was right below him. There was not a road or cabin anywhere in sight. When he landed he would be miles from civilization.

Branches snapped and leaves rustled loudly as Stoneman hit the treetops. His chute tangled in a moss-laden cypress tree. He hung help-lessly, dangling above the stagnant, foul-smelling water.

"I've got to cut myself loose," he muttered. Then, prying a knife from his back pocket, he did just that, hacking away at the lines until he plunged out of the trees toward the swamp.

"What the . . . ?" Stoneman cried as his de-scent came to an abrupt halt.

Something had broken his fall before he hit the water. Now he bounced up and down on a huge net of some sort. He tried to lift himself out of it, but couldn't.

"It's not a net at all," he realized. "It's a web. And I'm stuck to it!"

Stoneman thrashed and kicked until he was exhausted. Then as he lay still, trying to catch his breath, he saw it—the biggest vermula spider he had ever seen in his life—coming straight for him.

The huge black and brown spider inched its way across the sticky web. It stared hungrily at Stoneman, its pointed fangs bared, dripping its paralyzing liquid.

Stoneman kicked wildly, hoping to scare the murderous spider away.

But it kept coming . . . coming . . .

"Aaaaaahhhhhh!" Stoneman screamed as the vermula's huge fangs punctured his skin. He felt his body suddenly go cold, then numb. He'd been paralyzed.

The colossal spider crawled back and forth across the banker's body, spinning a thick, sticky cocoon over him. In minutes Stoneman was entombed in a coffin of suffocating white thread!

Weeks later an airplane pilot spotted the wreckage of Stoneman's plane while passing over the Okefenokee Swamp. It took the search party almost three weeks after that to hack its way through the swamp and discover Maxwell Stoneman's body.

"What is it?" one of the men shouted.

"He's nothing but a dried-up shell!" another cried in disgust. "It looks like everything's been . . . sucked out of his body."

"Ugh! What could have done it?" the first man wondered.

"Probably ants," said the leader. "C'mon, let's get out of here."

The party hadn't gotten far when one of the men fell behind.

"Hey, you guys! Wait up!" he called. "I'm caught on something."

The others turned and gasped. In seconds they were scattering through the slippery muck of the swamp, afraid to even glance back.

"Where are you guys going?" he called, picking at the thick gluey white threads that kept him rooted in place.

And then he heard it—a strange rustling sound coming from right behind him. . . .

Talk about a sticky situation, eh, kiddies? Oh, what a tangled web we weave. . . . Fangs for the memories, Mr. Stoneman!

Here's a mouth-watering favorite of mine. They say everything is relative. After you've read this gruesome tale of fetid family members, I'm sure you'll agree.

MOURNIN' AMBROSE

Standing on the shadowy front porch, Andrew Demert lifted the rusted door knocker and rapped it against the heavy, forbidding door. A hollow boom echoed through the cavernous mansion, replaced a moment later by the sound of shuffling feet.

The door emitted a high, creaking squeal as it opened, and a wrinkled face peered through a two-inch crack.

"Are . . . are you my uncle Ambrose Hawley?" Andrew asked, hoping it wasn't true.

The old man's eyes lit up and a wide grin stretched across his shriveled face. Uncle Ambrose swung the door open and extended his arms as wide as his unsettling grin.

"That's me!" he exclaimed with a pulsing

excitement that would have seemed impossible from the old man just seconds before. "You must be Andrew, my nephew! Come in!"

A moment later a leathery old woman shuffled into the foyer. Her gray hair was loosely pulled back into a bun. She was so hunched over she would have fallen on her face had it not been for the cane she carried.

"Who's *that?*" she cawed, her teeth rattling.

"You remember Andrew, don't you?" Ambrose said calmly. "He's going to stay with us awhile. Andrew, this is your aunt Elsa."

The old woman's face went white as a ghost. Her eyes grew wide with unmistakable terror.

"My sister Stella's boy? Has it come to that?"

"Please, Elsa," Ambrose said quietly. He glanced at Andrew. "She hasn't been . . . well lately—"

"They're all dead!" Aunt Elsa shrieked. "Three of them. Out there in the mausoleum."

"Elsa," Ambrose commanded, "go to the library. We'll be there momentarily."

"What's she talking about?" Andrew asked, confused.

His uncle dismissed his wife's ranting with a wave of his hand. The old woman grunted angrily and shuffled out of the foyer, disappearing through a narrow doorway.

"She's not well *here*," Uncle Ambrose announced, tapping the side of his head with a crooked finger. "Ever since the first death . . ."

"The first *death?*" Andrew said, not sure he'd heard right.

Uncle Ambrose seemed apologetic. "Of course, you couldn't have known. It happened three years ago, when we first moved here. One of your distant cousins came to stay with us. Lovely woman. She . . . died in her sleep."

"I—I didn't hear about it. There were other deaths?"

"Two others," Uncle Ambrose said. "My aged brother came to stay with us about two years ago. He passed away about a month later. Then my only niece came. It was tragic. . . . Such a young girl. . . ." He shook his head sadly. "Elsa took the first two hard, but the last, well . . . something just cracked . . ."

"You mean she's crazy?"

"Shhhhh!" Uncle Ambrose hissed. "Not crazy, really, just a little overdramatic. She tends to exaggerate."

They strolled through the dusty foyer into the library. There were books from wall to wall, floor to ceiling. None of them looked as though they'd been dusted in twenty years.

"This is a fantastic library," Andrew said, glancing around the room.

He turned and was startled by Aunt Elsa's wrinkled face staring at him not more than a foot away. "Like to read?" she said.

"Of course," he gulped, taking a giant step backward. "I go to college. I'm studying to be a writer."

"Ever read *Macbeth?* Where it says, 'Murder will out'?" She stared at him through tired, sagging eyes.

"N-no . . ." Andrew stuttered.

"Elsa, *please,*" Ambrose said, grabbing Andrew by the arm and leading him out to the hallway. "Come with me, Andrew. I'll show you to your room."

They climbed the wide marble stairs and walked the entire length of a dimly lit hallway. Ambrose stopped in front of a door and pushed it open.

"I'm sure you're tired after such a long journey. I hope you'll be comfortable here."

Andrew smiled. "I'm sure I will," he said, and bid his uncle good night.

Andrew paced about the room, still a little shaken by the sight of his deranged old aunt staring at him and telling him to read *Macbeth.* He crouched before a gigantic fireplace, struck a match, and touched it to the wood piled on the andirons. As the fire began to crackle and glow brightly, Andrew heard a strange thumping sound coming from behind him. A chill ran down the back of his neck. He stared into the reddish-blue glow of the flames, afraid to look behind him. When he did he almost fell into the blazing fire.

Aunt Elsa was shuffling toward him, her cane thumping against the wooden floor.

Andrew rose, his heart thumping ten times faster than her cane.

"I've come to warn you, Andrew," she said, her voice quivering. "Get out! Get out of this house and never come back. He's a fiend . . . a despicable fiend!"

"Uncle Ambrose?"

"Yes. I mustn't let it happen again. It's too horrible to imagine. You must leave at once! He's . . . he's . . ."

A shadow suddenly loomed across Aunt Elsa's face.

"Elsa! Get to bed this minute!" Uncle Ambrose roared.

"Y-yes, Ambrose," said Aunt Elsa. "I-I'm going." She turned and looked into Andrew's eyes pleadingly. "Remember, Andrew. 'Murder will out.'"

Andrew tossed and turned most of the night, more confused than ever. What was his aunt warning him about? The memory of her face, pallid and filled with fright, haunted him. And that phrase she had uttered so mysteriously, "Murder will out." What did it mean?

Loud, furious knocking woke him from what seemed like a very brief sleep. Andrew struggled to rouse himself. Bright morning sunlight poured in through cracks in the heavy curtains, searing his eyes.

"Andrew! Andrew!" Uncle Ambrose called frantically. "Come quickly! It's Aunt Elsa . . ."

Andrew jumped out of bed. He swung open the door and came face to face with Uncle Ambrose. Tears were streaming down the old man's face, and his decrepit body trembled.

"Uncle Ambrose, what's happened?"

"It's Elsa," his uncle sobbed. "She . . . she's
. . . *dead!*"

Aunt Elsa's funeral two days later was a lonely,
somber affair. An old priest from the town clos-
est to the Hawley estate presided over the short
ceremony. Afterward, her coffin was carried
out to the family mausoleum.

Andrew had hoped to leave the day after the
funeral but worried about Uncle Ambrose. The
old man barely talked anymore. At dinner his
plate went untouched. Each night Andrew
watched sadly as his uncle descended the wind-
ing stone pathway that led from the back of the
house to the mausoleum.

"Poor old guy," Andrew thought. "He
really misses her."

After watching Uncle Ambrose take his evening walk to the mausoleum, Andrew wan-
dered restlessly into the library. His eyes
scanned the library walls, looking at the endless
titles that could barely be read through the
thick dust covering them. The leather spine of
one book, however, was as dust-free as if it had
been printed yesterday.

The title was *Macbeth*.

Have you ever read . . . Macbeth . . . ?

Andrew could almost hear his aunt's quivering, pleading voice calling to him.

Murder will out . . .

He pulled down the book, opened it, and recognized his aunt's weak, scratchy handwriting. It was her diary! That's what she had been trying to tell him—she had wanted him to read her diary!

The handwriting was sloppy, almost unintelligible, but gradually he was able to make out certain words. *Ambrose . . . Suffocation . . . Murder . . .* Soon he could read whole sentences, and what he read terrified him.

Andrew slapped the book shut and shuddered. He had to talk to the police.

Chief Inspector Spencer listened quietly as Andrew read aloud from his aunt's diary. The inspector's assistant, Detective Kelly, thoughtfully twisted his perfectly formed handlebar mustache in silence.

". . . And this one, Inspector, listen to this. 'I know how he murdered them. Suffocation! He drugged them so they couldn't resist, then

76

smothered them with a pillow.' But, why? Why?"

Inspector Spencer glanced at his assistant, but his stern face showed no emotion.

"Here's the last passage," Andrew went on. "'Andrew has arrived today. He will be next! I must warn him. The fiend will do to him what he has done to the others. If Ambrose were to find out that I mean to tell Andrew everything, he would certainly kill me.'"

The inspector's bushy eyebrows arched grimly. "And you say Ambrose interrupted Elsa that night as she was about to tell you something?"

Andrew nodded. "Still, one thing puzzles me. If he murdered her, why does he mourn her?"

"*Murdered* her?" Detective Kelly scoffed. "The doctor called it a natural death."

"Suffocation looks like a natural death!" Andrew cried, rising angrily from his chair.

"The only way to prove that she was murdered, Mr. Demert, is to get permission from your uncle to disinter the body and perform an autopsy," said the inspector.

The next day Andrew watched from high atop the staircase as the two police detectives spoke to Uncle Ambrose, telling him they wanted to disinter Aunt Elsa.

"Never! Never!" Uncle Ambrose cried.

"If you refuse, Mr. Hawley, we can get a court order giving us permission," Inspector Spencer replied.

"Please, you have no right to disturb her," Ambrose sobbed. "She's been laid to rest. Leave her alone."

The two detectives glanced at each other, then bid Ambrose good-bye. Andrew hurried down a back staircase and met them before they got into their car.

"What are you going to do?" he asked.

"Just stay calm," said Detective Kelly.

Inspector Spencer placed his hat on his head. "And keep an eye on him, Demert. We'll be in touch."

That night, when Uncle Ambrose put on his overcoat and walked out the door of the mansion, Andrew followed. He trailed his uncle's shadowy figure as it descended the sloping path, crossed the neglected garden, and entered the mausoleum.

Andrew crept silently along the edge of the small stone building until he stood directly outside its partially open door. He listened a moment but heard nothing. Shouldn't his uncle be crying or talking gently to his recently deceased wife, telling her that he missed her and would someday be with her?

Andrew was wondering about all these things when he peered into the darkened tomb from behind a stone pillar.

A moan almost escaped his throat. He placed a trembling hand over his mouth and stumbled as far away from the tomb as he could. He stopped at a tree, gagging violently.

Then he heard footsteps beside him.

"Demert, what's wrong?" Detective Kelly asked, alarmed at the sight of Andrew's deathly pale face.

"He's sick as a dog," said Spencer. "Demert, where's your uncle?"

"In the . . . tomb," Andrew managed to say. "Hurry!"

The two detectives burst through the door of the mausoleum. Uncle Ambrose was hunched over Aunt Elsa's coffin. When he saw them, the old man growled at the intruders.

"Get out!" he snarled.

Behind him was the partially eaten corpse of his wife. Chunks of her dead flesh had been ripped from her body. The demented old man's skeletal hands were reaching for more . . .

"He's a ghoul!" Kelly cried in horror. "He's a sick fiend, just like the old lady's diary said—"

"Grab him!" the inspector yelled, lunging at the ghastly old man.

Several other police officers rushed into the tomb, shackled the wildly screaming man, and carted him away.

"What made you come back?" Andrew asked the detectives shakily.

"A hunch," said Spencer. "We talked to the undertaker back in town. He told us that your uncle never let him embalm any of the bodies. That's when we knew something was wrong. The other bodies in the tomb have been stripped of their flesh, too."

Andrew gagged.

"You okay, Demert?" Inspector Spencer asked.

"A little wobbly," Andrew admitted. He shuddered and shook his head. "But at least I'm not going to be a seven-course meal for that hideous old man."

Well, at least young Andrew will have something interesting to write about in his creative writing class. I heard he became a vegetarian that very day . . . !

 *Gather 'round, kiddies. It's time for the final story of my fright-filled fun fest. I've saved the most hideous, disgusting, revolting, sickening story for last. I know—you're thinking it couldn't get worse than that last lurid tale. Wanna bet?*

THE THING FROM THE GRAVE

"Don't worry about a thing, honey," Jim Barry said from the driver's seat of his convertible. "I'll be back by tomorrow night at the latest."

He reached out and wiped a tear from his wife's cheek and smiled reassuringly. The handsome young couple had been married less than a month, and during that time they had been inseparable. Now business was calling Jim away for the first time, and his wife Laura was worried.

"Jim, I'm afraid," she said, biting her lower lip. "I don't want to be left alone. What if Bill . . ."

"Bill again?" Jim thought ruefully. "Laura, please," he said. "Bill isn't going to do anything

82

to you. By now I'm sure he knows it's just you and me."

"But you know how . . . persistent . . . he can be," Laura said nervously. "He's the world's worst loser."

Persistent was an understatement, Jim thought. Bill Ferth had been in love with Laura for years. After Laura had accepted Jim's proposal to marry him, Bill was furious. Just before the wedding, Jim and Laura had run into him at a restaurant in town. While he said all the right things, Jim saw something sinister lurking in Bill's beady eyes. Something that scared him.

"Laura, listen to me," Jim said gravely. He clutched his wife's hand and gave it a firm squeeze. "If you're ever in any danger, I'll be there to help you. No matter where I am, somehow, some way, I'll get to you. I'll save you. I promise."

Laura frowned. "Don't mock me, Jim. Just please, please hurry back." She waved sadly as his sleek new convertible pulled out of the driveway and disappeared into the night.

It bothered Jim that Laura was still frightened of Bill. Feeling guilty about leaving his beautiful wife alone, he thought of the promise he'd made, wondering if he'd be able to keep it if he ever had to . . .

No matter where I am, somehow, some way, I'll get to you. I'll save you. I promise . . .

"What the—!"

A figure darted into the road in front of his convertible. Jim slammed his foot down hard against the brake and the car squealed to a halt.

"Are you nuts?" Jim shouted angrily at the figure standing in his headlight beams. "I could have killed you!"

"Jim, it's me," the man yelled, coming toward the car. "Bill."

Bill? Jim was alarmed.

"What's he doing out here in the middle of no—"

A flash of metal in Bill's hand glinted in the headlight beams as he approached the car. Bill was smiling, trying to appear friendly, but Jim could see that sinister something in his eyes. Just then another flash, and Jim saw . . .

. . . a knife!

It came up in a blur and plunged down again and again, violently. Jim threw up his arms and screamed, but it was the last sound he would ever make.

Bill stared down at Jim's body slumped lifelessly over the steering wheel.

"Now Laura will be all mine," he said hoarsely. "All mine . . ."

By the time Bill had dragged Jim's body far into the woods his breathing was so labored he thought he might have a heart attack. His throat ached and his heart pounded crazily in his chest.

Worse, he still had a hole to dig.

His shovel cut into the hard, unyielding dirt with a clang. The digging was more difficult than he thought, and he stopped after a few minutes. He'd always heard that graves were supposed to be six feet deep, but he decided to make an exception in this case.

"Sorry, old buddy," Bill said with a chuckle. "Three feet is all you're going to get. I always thought you were a shallow person, Jim."

Bill's hysterical laughter cut through the blackness of the dense forest as he placed the heel of a muddy shoe against Jim's stiffening body and rolled it into the dank burial pit. Ex-

cept for a deer and a few late-night chipmunks, his insane cackles were heard by no one.

Then he drove Jim's convertible up to Lookout Canyon, placed a heavy rock on the gas pedal, and cheered as the car tumbled end over end down the cliff, then splashed heavily into the water below.

Jim's brand-new car bubbled and gurgled as it pitched lazily at the surface, then sank deep into the bottom of the lake.

Laura rushed to the door at the first knock, her heart leaping with anticipation. Was it Jim, back after disappearing mysteriously for more than a month?

She swung open the door. But when she saw Bill standing there, her heart sank lower than before, something she had thought would be impossible.

"Bill, what are you doing here?" she said weakly.

"Some greeting," Bill replied arrogantly, stepping into the living room without being asked. He lit a cigarette and blew a stream of smoke into the air. "I heard through the grapevine that Jim left you for another woman. I could have told you he was capable of something as low as that."

"Get out!" Laura cried furiously. "Jim would never do anything like that. Something's happened to him. I know it. I feel it. Get out of my house!"

Bill waltzed out confidently. "I'll be back," he thought as the door slammed behind him. "Pretty soon she'll realize her mistake and forget that jerk. Then she'll be mine."

Another month passed. Bill had secretly been watching Laura every day, and this evening he would make his move. He had to convince her that *he* was the one who loved her. This time he wouldn't take no for an answer.

"What are you doing here?" Laura cried when she found Bill at her door again. "Please go away. I don't want to see you."

"Listen to me, Laura," said Bill as he walked through her doorway, flicking cigarette ashes on the floor. "Jim's gone. He's never coming back. If something had happened to him, you would have heard by now. Face it. He left you, can't you see that? Deserted you!"

Laura sobbed. Tears rolled down the smooth skin of her cheeks. She knew in her heart that Jim would never leave her like that. Never!

"I'll wait for him," she declared. "He's coming back. And I'll wait for him. Even if it takes forever—"

Bill threw his cigarette to the floor and ground it out angrily. "He's never coming back!" he screamed. *"Never!"*

"I'll always love him, Bill. Jim was my life. Without him—"

"Then it's all wasted . . ." Bill mumbled. A sickening realization hit him like a truck. He could never make Laura change her mind. The thought infuriated him. "All the planning . . . the work . . . the waiting . . . wasted."

"What are you talking about?" Laura said. "What do you mean, planning? Are you saying—"

"Yes!" he growled. "I killed him. I wanted you, Laura, and he stood in my way!"

Laura backed away, fear and disgust on her face. "Y-you killed Jim? I hate you! You . . . you maniac!" she screamed.

"That does it. You're coming with me," Bill told her. "If I can't have you, then no one will. I'm going to kill you." And with that he forced

Laura into his car and drove her to a deserted cabin deep in the woods, not far from where he had buried Jim. Grabbing her by the arm, he led her inside.

"What are you going to do?" Laura asked fearfully. "Please let me go. Please . . ."

"I'm going to lock you in and set fire to the cabin. They'll never find what's left of you. This place will be nothing more than a mountain of ashes—yours included."

Bill slammed the door and locked it, leaving Laura alone in the pitch-black room. She frantically tried the door handle, then pounded on the door. It was useless. Where was Jim now? she wondered sadly, her mind shrinking from the thought of a fiery death. "Please, Jim," she cried silently, "you promised. You promised you'd save me."

Then she began to scream out loud. Her earsplitting cry cut through the still, black night.

"Eeeaaagghh!"

"Scream all you like," Bill called mockingly from outside. *"No one will hear you!"*

But something *did* hear Laura's cries. Somewhere far out in the woods it stirred. Suddenly, inexplicably, the ground moved. Dirt gave way, rocks and leaves were pushed aside, and *something* clawed its way to the surface.

Suddenly a hand—or what looked like a hand—burst out of the ground. The nubs of its fingers were nothing more than white bone. Strands of flesh hung from its knuckles like hideous strings of spaghetti. The barely recognizable claw grasped at the side of the grave, pulling, pulling . . .

"Eeeaaagghh!"

Laura's voice careened through the night, reached the pulsating earth, and seemed to give life to whatever was beneath the soil.

A rotted human head oozed from the pit. Patches of torn flesh crawling with worms

clung to the skull, which grinned a hideous dead man's grin. The cool air energized the horribly mangled *thing*, filling it with enough strength to struggle out of the grave and stand on its own rotting feet.

As Laura's desperate cries continued, the thing took a lurching, staggering stride in her direction.

Not far away, Bill finished dousing the cabin with kerosene, then tossed the empty can into the woods and struck a match. In a *whooosh!* the fragrant trail of liquid was transformed into a blue line of flames that ringed the building and leaped up the walls. In a matter of seconds the whole cabin crackled and smoked.

Laura's terrified screams grew louder, her pounding more frantic. Then all the noise from inside stopped. Bill stepped back from the tremendous heat of the blaze as though admiring a work of art.

He was staring at the flames curling up from the cabin, when he suddenly had the feeling that someone—or something—was watching him. He turned and looked toward the edge of the clearing.

"*Oh, my God!*" he gasped.

In the fluttering orange light of the blaze Bill saw the Thing—it could not really be called a man, although it walked on two legs and wore the tattered remnants of clothing—stumbling toward the cabin.

The Thing burst through the locked door, stepped inside, and was engulfed in flames. In a corner the Thing found Laura, unconscious, curled up in the only part of the room that was not ravaged by the deadly fire.

The Thing picked her up and quickly passed through the flames to the safety of the clearing. There it set her down on a soft cool bed of leaves. Behind them the cabin was crumbling, its charred embers glowing orange and red. Laura stirred, her blurred vision seeing only the silhouette of a figure standing over her.

"Jim?" she thought groggily, just barely conscious.

Suddenly the Thing turned its charred skull in Bill's direction.

Bill saw it looking hungrily at him. "Jim?" he thought, dumbstruck.

Bill screamed and bolted through the woods. The Thing followed relentlessly.

"Help, somebody!" Bill cried. He ran and ran, desperate to put some distance between himself and that horrible . . . thing.

He paused at a giant oak, breathing heavily. Was there any sound that might tell him the thing was near? No. Only the sweet whisper of leaves rustling in the wind, of thousands of bugs chirping as they did every night.

Bill tried to get his bearings. He knew the woods around here, and this area seemed familiar.

"Yes," he thought, "that way, and I'll be out at the road in a matter of minutes." He took a deep breath and rushed away from the tree, only to tumble headfirst into a shallow hole in the ground.

"It's—it's where I buried Jim," Bill realized. "It's his grave!"

The sound of shuffling feet almost stopped Bill's heart from beating. He turned over and was met by the most horrifying sight of his life: the Thing—Jim's decaying body—was hovering over him.

"Noooooooooo!" Bill screamed as the Thing tumbled down on top of him, its eyeless sockets inches from his face, its stench like death's own perfume.

Bill writhed and screamed, but the awful thing held him down as it shoveled earth over both of them. In seconds the dirt was up to Bill's neck . . . in his mouth . . . his nose. Bill's gurgling screams became muffled moans as the dirt came down over his face.

There was no one in the deep, dense forest to hear Bill's terrified screaming as he was buried alive. And there was no one there to hear it when it stopped, either. . . .

Poor Jim was just <u>dying</u> for some company.
Now he'll have someone to talk to for eternity.
I'll bet he and Bill will enjoy lots of <u>grave</u>
conversations. But remember, boys, no <u>dirty</u> words
. . . Heh! Heh! Heh!